For Mum and Dad with love

ISBN 1 85854 695 8
Published by Brimax Books Ltd, Newmarket,
England, CB8 7AU 1998.
Printed in Spain.

The Itsy Bitsy Spider

Compiled and Illustrated by Jenny Press

BRIMAX • NEWMARKET • ENGLAND

Introduction

Mothers and fathers sing children's songs, recite nursery rhymes, and repeat children's verses - frequently those they remember from their childhood - to their own children almost from birth. Most children, before they even learn to speak, have heard dozens of rhymes, songs and verses. As the child grows he or she learns the skills of language, articulation and memory in part by repeating the songs, nursery rhymes and snatches of verse learned from parents and other children.

Nursery rhymes can even be considered - looking on to the pre-school and primary years - as an introduction to more classic forms of verse. In this selection we have put together nursery rhymes, childhood rhymes, and some simple poems so that as the child grows, he or she may progress on to more complex - yet still simple - language skills. And most importantly, both children and parents can have a lot of fun learning the rhymes and verses that are an important part of what it is to be a child.

Contents

A wee little worm in a hickory-nut
Sang, happy as he could be,
"O, I live in the heart of the whole round world,
And it all belongs to me!"
(James Whitcomb Riley)

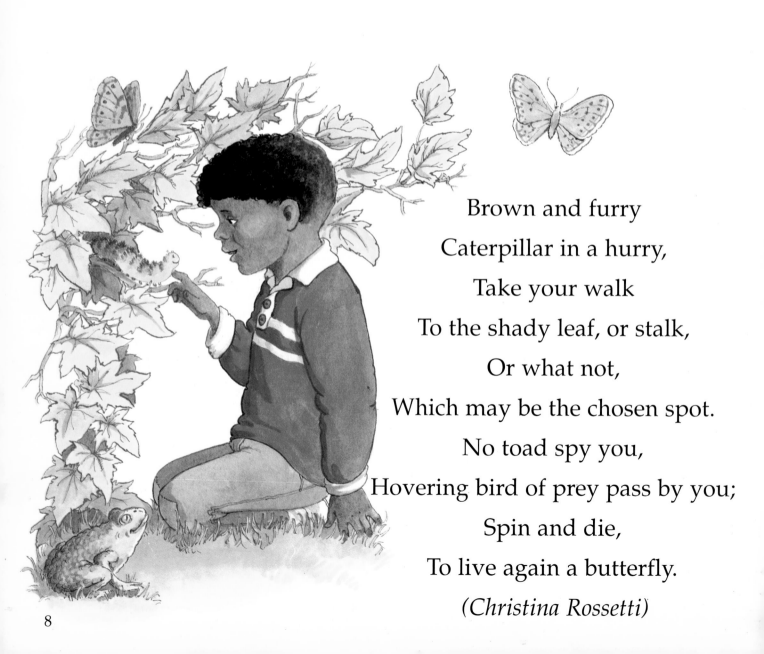

Brown and furry
Caterpillar in a hurry,
Take your walk
To the shady leaf, or stalk,
Or what not,
Which may be the chosen spot.
No toad spy you,
Hovering bird of prey pass by you;
Spin and die,
To live again a butterfly.
(Christina Rossetti)

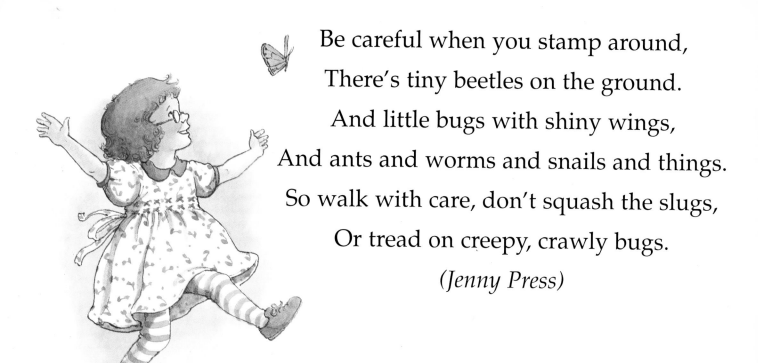

Be careful when you stamp around,
There's tiny beetles on the ground.
And little bugs with shiny wings,
And ants and worms and snails and things.
So walk with care, don't squash the slugs,
Or tread on creepy, crawly bugs.

(Jenny Press)

The itsy bitsy spider
Went up the water spout,
Down came the rain
And washed the spider out.

Out came the sun,
And dried up all the rain,
And the itsy bitsy spider
Went up the spout again.

(Traditional)

9

Mary, Mary, quite contrary,
How does your garden grow?
With silver bells and cockle shells,
And pretty maids all in a row.
(Traditional)

Roses are red,
Violets are blue,
Sugar is sweet
And so are you.
(Traditional)

Lavender's blue, dilly, dilly,
Lavender's green;
When I am King, dilly, dilly,
You shall be Queen.
(Traditional)

One, two, three, four,
Mary at the cottage door,
Five, six, seven, eight,
Eating cherries off a plate.
(Traditional)

Look out! Look out!
Jack Frost is about!
He's after our fingers and toes;
And, all through the night
The gay, little sprite
Is working where nobody knows.
(Cecily Pike)

Rain on the green grass,
And rain on the tree,
Rain on the house-top
But not on me!
(Anon)

When I was down beside the sea,
A wooden spade they gave to me
To dig the sandy shore.
My holes were empty like a cup,
In every hole the sea came up,
Till it could come no more.

(Robert Louis Stevenson)

Little wind, blow on the hill-top;
Little wind, blow down the plain;
Little wind, blow up the sunshine,
Little wind, blow off the rain.

(Kate Greenaway)

Pat-a-cake, pat-a-cake, baker's man
Bake me a cake as fast as you can;
Pat it and prick it and mark it with B,
Put it in the oven for baby and me.

(Traditional)

Hot cross buns!
Hot cross buns!
One a penny, two a penny,
Hot cross buns!

(Traditional)

14

Handy Spandy, Jack-a-Dandy,
Loves plum cake and sugar candy;
He brought some at a grocer's shop,
And out he came, hop, hop, hop, hop.
(Traditional)

Polly put the kettle on,
Polly put the kettle on,
Polly put the kettle on,
We'll all have tea.
Sukey take it off again,
Sukey take it off again,
Sukey take it off again,
They've all gone away.
(Traditional)

Fuzzy Wuzzy was a bear,
A bear was Fuzzy Wuzzy.
When Fuzzy Wuzzy lost his hair
He wasn't fuzzy, was he?
(Anon)

Teddy bear cannot be seen
Until his face is nice and clean.
My teddy nearly always cries
Because the soap goes in his eyes.
(Anon)

Teddy bear, teddy bear turn around.
Teddy bear, teddy bear touch the ground.
Teddy bear, teddy bear go up stairs.
Teddy bear, teddy bear say your prayers.
Teddy bear, teddy bear switch off the light.
Teddy bear, teddy bear say good night.
(Anon)

Round and round the garden,

Like a teddy bear,

One step, two step…

Tickle you under there!

(Traditional)

Diddlety, diddlety, dumpty
The cat ran up the plum tree;
Half a crown to get her down
Diddlety, diddlety, dumpty.
(Traditional)

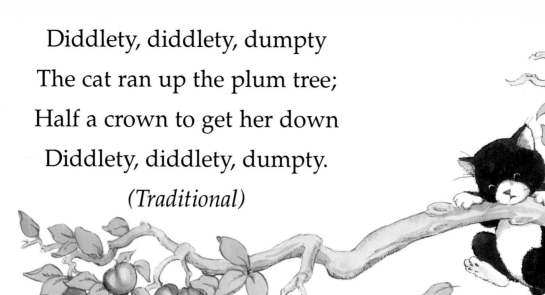

Ding, dong, bell,
Pussy's in the well.
Who put her in?
Little Johnny Green.
Who pulled her out?
Little Tommy Stout.
What a naughty boy was that,
To try to drown poor pussy cat.
(Traditional)

There once were two cats from Kilkenny
Each thought there was one cat too many.
So they fought and they fit,
And they scratched and they bit,
'Till excepting their nails
And the tips of their tails
Instead of two cats there weren't any.
(Traditional)

Sally go round the sun,
Sally go round the moon,
Sally go round the chimney pots
On a Saturday afternoon.
(Traditional)

Here am I,
Little jumping Joan;
When nobody's with me
I'm all alone.
(Traditional)

Jack be nimble,
Jack be quick,
Jack jump over
The candlestick.
(Traditional)

Late on a dark and stormy night,
Three witches stirred with all their might.
Two little ghosts said, "How d'ye do?"
The wizard went tiptoe, tiptoe,
BOO!
(Anon)

One-eyed Jack, the pirate chief,
Was a terrible, fearsome, ocean thief.
He wore a peg
Upon one leg;
He wore a hook -
And a dirty look!
One-eyed Jack, the pirate chief,
Was a terrible, fearsome, ocean thief.
(Anon)

When Barney and me built the house in the tree,
We wanted to stay there forever.
But Barney took fright at the dark and the night,
So we held hands and ran home together.
(Jenny Press)

In the dark, dark wood, there was a dark, dark house,
And in that dark, dark house, there was a dark, dark room,
And in that dark, dark room, there was a dark, dark shelf,
And on that dark, dark shelf, there was a dark, dark box,
And in that dark, dark box, there was a … GHOST!

(Anon)

Little Boy Blue
Come blow your horn,
The sheep's in the meadow,
The cow's in the corn;
But where is the boy
Who looks after the sheep?
He's under the haystack,
Fast asleep.
(Traditional)

Jack and Jill went up the hill
To fetch a pail of water;
Jack fell down and broke his crown,
And Jill came tumbling after.
(Traditional)

Tom, Tom, the piper's son,
Stole a pig and away he run;
The pig was eat
And Tom was beat,
And Tom went howling
Down the street.
(Traditional)

Little Bo Peep has lost her sheep,
And can't tell where to find them;
Leave them alone,
And they'll come home,
And bring their tails behind them.
(Traditional)

Sleep baby, sleep,

Our cottage vale is deep:

The little lamb is on the green,

With woolly fleece so soft and clean –

Sleep baby, sleep.

(Anon)

All day long

The sun shines bright.

The moon and stars

Come out by night.

From twilight time

They line the skies

And watch the world

With quiet eyes.

(Anon)

Golden slumbers kiss your eyes,

Smiles awake you when you rise.

Sleep pretty baby, do not cry,

And I will sing a lullaby.

(*Thomas Dekker*)

Jack Sprat could eat no fat,

His wife could eat no lean.

And so between them both, you see,

They licked the platter clean.

(Traditional)

Old Mother Hubbard

Went to the cupboard,

To fetch her poor dog a bone;

But when she got there

The cupboard was bare

And so the poor dog had none.

(Traditional)

Monday's child is fair of face,
Tuesday's child is full of grace,
Wednesday's child is full of woe,
Thursday's child has far to go,
Friday's child works hard for a living,
Saturday's child is loving and giving;
But the child that is born on the sabbath day,
Is bonny and blithe and good and gay.

(*Traditional*)

Way down south where bananas grow,
A grasshopper stepped on an elephant's toe.
The elephant said, with tears in his eyes,
"Pick on somebody your own size."
(Anon)

There was an Old Person of Ware,
Who rode on the back of a Bear,
When they asked, "Does it trot?"
He said, "Certainly not!
He's a Moppsikon Floppsikon Bear!"
(Edward Lear)

If you should meet a crocodile,
Don't take a stick and poke him;
Ignore the welcome in his smile,
Be careful not to stroke him.

For as he sleeps upon the Nile,
He thinner gets and thinner;
And whene'er you meet a crocodile
He's ready for his dinner.
(Anon)

There was an old woman
Tossed up in a basket,
Seventeen times as high as the moon;
Where she was going
I couldn't but ask it,
For in her hand she carried a broom.

(Traditional)

Dickory, dickory, dare,
The pig flew into the air;
The man in brown
Soon brought her down,
Dickory, dickory, dare.

(Traditional)

Hey diddle diddle,

The cat and the fiddle,

The cow jumped over the moon;

The little dog laughed

To see such sport,

And the dish ran away with the spoon.

(Traditional)

Old Mother Goose

When she wanted to wander

Would ride through the air

On a very fine gander.

(Traditional)

The grizzly and the polar bears
    Were friendly as can be,
So they ate their lunch together
With a sandwich on each knee.
        (Gill Davies)

Nobody loves me,
    Everybody hates me,
I think I'll go and eat worms.
    Great, big, fat ones,
    Long, thin, skinny ones,
See how the little one squirms.
        (Anon)

I eat my peas with honey;
I've done it all my life:
It makes the peas taste funny,
But it keeps them on the knife.

(Anon)

Jelly on a plate,
Jelly on a plate,
Wibble, wobble, wibble, wobble,
Jelly on a plate.

(Anon)

See-saw, Margery Daw,
Jacky shall have a new master;
Jacky shall have but a penny a day,
Because he can't work any faster.
(Traditional)

Boys and girls
Come out to play,
The moon doth shine
As bright as day.
Leave your supper
And leave your sleep,
And join your playfellows
In the street.
(Traditional)

Ring-a-ring o'roses,
A pocket full of posies,
A-tishoo! A-tishoo!
We all fall down.
(Traditional)

Georgy Porgy, pudding and pie,
Kissed the girls and made them cry.
And when the boys came out to play,
Georgy Porgy ran away.
(Traditional)

There was an old owl who lived in an oak;
The more he heard, the less he spoke.
The less he spoke, the more he heard.
Why aren't we like that wise old bird?
(Anon)

I have a dog and his name is Rags,
He eats so much that his tummy sags,
His ears flip-flop,
And his tail wig-wags,
And when he walks he goes zig-zag.
(Anon)

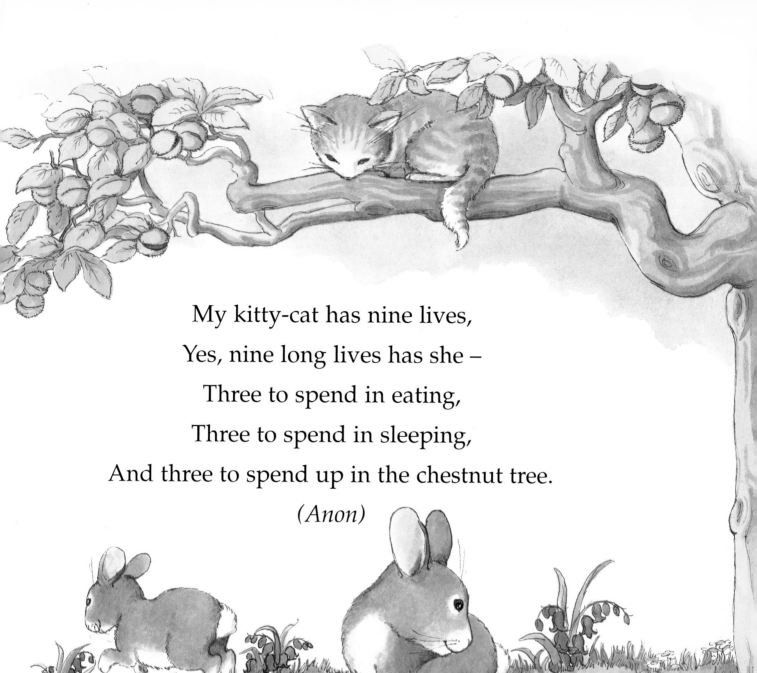

My kitty-cat has nine lives,

Yes, nine long lives has she –

Three to spend in eating,

Three to spend in sleeping,

And three to spend up in the chestnut tree.

(Anon)

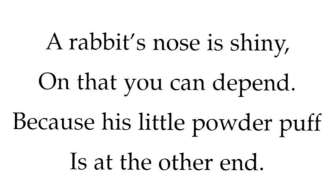

A rabbit's nose is shiny,

On that you can depend.

Because his little powder puff

Is at the other end.

(Anon)

Ride a cock-horse
To Banbury Cross,
To see a fine lady
Upon a white horse;
With rings on her fingers
And bells on her toes,
She shall have music
Wherever she goes.
(Traditional)

Hark, hark,
The dogs do bark,
The beggars are coming to town;
Some in rags,
And some in jags,
And one in a velvet gown.
(Traditional)

38

Daffy down dilly is coming to town
In a yellow petticoat and a green gown.
(Traditional)

Little Tommy Tucker
Sings for his supper.
What shall we give him?
White bread and butter.
How shall he cut it
Without a knife?
How will he be married
Without a wife?
(Traditional)

Swinging on a gate, swinging on a gate,
Seven little sisters and a brother makes eight.
Seven pretty pinafores and one bow tie,
Fourteen pigtails and one black eye.

Swinging on a gate, swinging on a gate,
Seven little sisters and a brother makes eight.
The school bell rings, and off they go –
Eight little children all in a row.

(Anon)

In jumping and tumbling
We spend the whole day,
Till night by arriving
Has finished our play.

What then? One and all,
There's no more to be said,
As we tumbled all day,
So we tumble to bed.

(Anon)

How do you like to go up in a swing,

Up in the air so blue?

Oh, I do think it the pleasantest thing

Ever a child can do!

Till I look down on the garden green,

Down on the roof so brown –

Up in the air I go flying again,

Up in the air and down!

(Robert Louis Stevenson)

Rock-a-bye, baby
On the tree top,
When the wind blows
The cradle will rock;
When the bough breaks
The cradle will fall,
And down will come baby,
Cradle, and all.

(Traditional)

Star light, star bright,
First star I see tonight;
I wish I may, I wish I might
Have the wish I wish tonight.

(Traditional)

Wee Willie Winkie
Runs through the town,
Upstairs and downstairs
In his night-gown,
Rapping at the window,
Crying through the lock,
Are the children all in bed,
For now it's eight o'clock?
(Traditional)

The man in the moon
Looked out of the moon,
Looked out of the moon and said,
"It's time for all the children on earth
To think about going to bed."
(Traditional)

Index of First Lines